S0-AXV-343

THE LITTLE COWBOY
AND
THE BIG COWBOY

M CP
Modern Curriculum Press
BEGINNING
TO
READ
Series

THE LITTLE COWBOY AND
THE BIG COWBOY

Margaret Hillert

Illustrated by Dan Siculan

MODERN CURRICULUM PRESS
Cleveland · Toronto

Library of Congress Cataloging in Publication Data

Hillert, Margaret.
  The little cowboy and the big cowboy.

  SUMMARY: A little cowboy and his father ride
horses, round up cattle, mend a fence, practice
roping, cook over a campfire, and sleep outdoors
in their sleeping bags.
  [1. Cowboys—Fiction] I. Siculan, Dan.
II. Title.
PZ7.H558Li   [E]   80–14566
ISBN 0-8136-5076-3 (hardbound)
ISBN 0-8136-5576-5 (paperback)

  3 4 5 6 7 8 9   88

Library of Congress Catalog Number: 80–14566

Here is a little cowboy.

And here is a big cowboy.

Here is something little
for the little cowboy.
It can go.
It can run.

7

Here is something big
for the big cowboy.
It can go.
It can run, too.

The two cowboys can ride.
It is fun to ride.
Fun to ride away.

But the two cowboys
have to work, too.
The little cowboy can
help the big cowboy.

10

Here is something to do.
Look here. Look here.
What do you see?

11

The big cowboy can get
the big ones.
That is good.

13

The little cowboy can get
the little ones.
That is good, too.

14

15

Oh, look here.
Something is down.
Here is work to do.

Work, work, work.

Make it good.

Now no one can get out.

Here is something that
is fun to do.
The big cowboy can do it.

But the little cowboy
can not do it.
The little cowboy will have
to work at it.

Oh, look at this.
How big it is!
Big, big, big.

And look at this.
Look what the cowboys see now.
How pretty it is.

23

The big cowboy will make
something to eat.
The little cowboy will work, too.

25

The big cowboy and the little
cowboy can eat now.
My, this is good.

Here is something cowboys like.
You can play it.
It is fun to play.

The little cowboy can
play a little one.
The big cowboy can
play a big one.

The little cowboy gets
down in here.
And the big cowboy gets
down in here.

The cowboys do not have
to work now.
This is good.
The cowboys like to do this.

Margaret Hillert, author of several books in the MCP Beginning-To-Read Series, is a writer, poet, and teacher.

The Little Cowboy and the Big Cowboy uses the 50 words listed below.

a	get(s)	make	see
and	go	my	something
at	good		
away		no	that
	have	not	the
big	help	now	this
but	here		to
	how	oh	too
can		one(s)	two
cowboy(s)	in	out	
	is		what
do	it	play	will
down		pretty	work
	like		
eat	little	ride	you
	look	run	
for			
fun